painting a wall

a hammer

a builder

Using this book

Ladybird's *talkabouts* are ideal for encouraging children to talk about what they see. Bold colourful pictures and simple questions help to develop early learning skills – such as matching, counting and detailed observation.

Look at this book with your child. First talk about the pictures yourself, and point out things to look at. Let your child take his* time. With encouragement, he will start to join in, talking about the familiar things in the pictures. Help him to count objects, to look for things that match, and to talk about what is going on in the picture stories.

To avoid the clumsy use of he/she, the child is referred to as 'he'. **talkabouts** *are suitable for both boys and girls.*

Published by Ladybird Books Ltd
80 Strand London WC2R ORL
A Penguin Company

3 5 7 9 10 8 6 4

© LADYBIRD BOOKS MMIII

Printed in Italy

talkabout
Building Site

written by Lorraine Horsley
illustrated by Alex Ayliffe

Ladybird

A building site is a busy place.
First the builders must clear
the site.
Talk about how they do this.

What do you think is going
to be built?

What are the vehicles on the building site doing?

Can you find...

digger

dumper truck

bulldozer

cement mixer

How many vehicles can you see?

9

Bill and Ben are bricklayers.
They build the walls.

Which wall is the highest?
Which wall is the lowest?

Ross and Raj are roofers.
They put tiles on the roof.
Who is higher up?
How many other houses can you see?

12

13

Accidents can happen on a building site, so the builders must wear hard hats, gloves and boots.

The builders have lost their gloves
and boots, can you help them
find them?

How many boots can you count?
How many gloves?

Jenny is a joiner. She builds stairs and cupboards and puts on doors.

What tools do you think Jenny
is using?

Match the tools to their shadows.

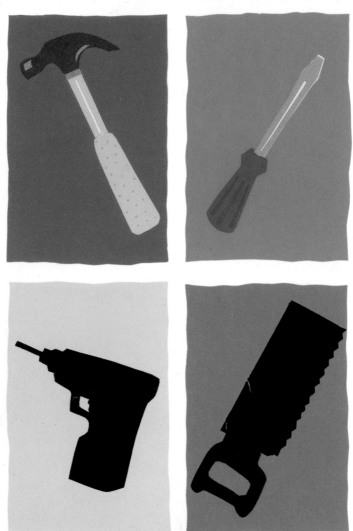

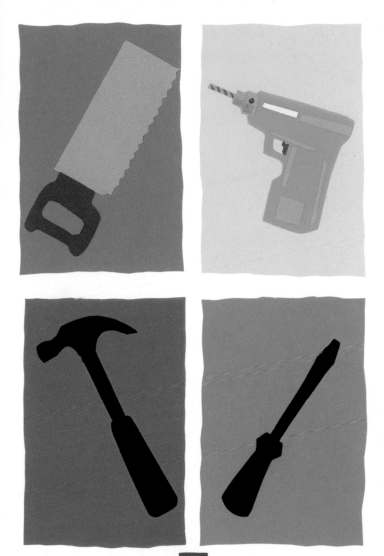

19

Pete is a plumber. He puts in the pipes that carry water round the house. Can you see what other things he puts in the house?

Find another...

tap

plug

toilet

Debbie is a decorator. She paints the house inside and out.
What colour is she painting the walls?

What other colour paints does
she have?

The house is finished. Can you find windows with these shapes?

circle

square

rectangle

diamond

SOLD

What shape is the front door?

It's moving day. Tell the story.

Can you find these as well?

a bulldozer

a sunflower

a green boot